SLY, P.I.

SLY, P. I.

THE CASE OF THE MISSING SHOES

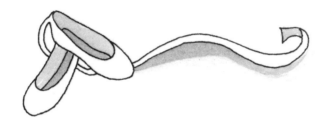

by
Cathy Stefanec-Ogren

illustrated by
Priscilla Posey Circolo

HARPER & ROW, PUBLISHERS

For those who believed in me,
Mom, Dad, Tom, and Beth

Sly, P.I.

Text copyright © 1989 by Cathy Stefanec-Ogren
Illustrations copyright © 1989 by Priscilla Posey Circolo

All rights reserved. No part of this book may be
used or reproduced in any manner whatsoever without
written permission except in the case of brief
quotations embodied in critical articles and reviews.
Printed in the United States of America.
For information address Harper & Row Junior Books,
10 East 53rd Street, New York, N.Y. 10022.
Published simultaneously in Canada by
Fitzhenry & Whiteside Limited, Toronto.
Typography by Andrew Rhodes
1   2   3   4   5   6   7   8   9   10

First Edition

Library of Congress Cataloging-in-Publication Data

Stefanec-Ogren, Cathy.
  Sly, P.I. / by Cathy Stefanec-Ogren;
illustrated by Priscilla Posey Circolo.—1st ed.
      p.   cm.
  Summary: When ballet star Lotta Oink's toe
shoes disappear on opening night, self-made fox and
old friend, Sly, P.I., solves the case.
  ISBN 0-06-024631-6 : $
  ISBN 0-06-024632-4 (lib. bdg.): $
  [1. Mystery and detective stories.   2. Ballet dancing
  —Fiction.   3. Pigs—Fiction.   4. Foxes—Fiction.]
  I. Circolo, Priscilla Posey, ill.   II. Title.   III. Title: Sly, PI.
PZ7.S8155S1 1989   87-29352
[E]—dc19   CIP
                                                          AC

Contents

Opening Night

· 1 ·

I am a self-made fox and proud of it. From the time I left the farm, my clever mind helped me solve many cases. I moved from town to town, city to city. I worked my way across the country, helping others. I became known as Sly, P.I.

That night, I was returning to my hometown to see an old friend. There was something in the air. It was not an ordinary night. But I am not an ordinary private investigator.

As I stepped out of the cab, I looked at
the sign above the Opera House.

I entered the Opera House with a box of her favorite chocolates in my hand. I made my way backstage. I found her practicing some steps with her partner.

· 9 ·

She jumped. She whirled. She spun.

She made a leap into the arms of the Russian wolfhound. I couldn't take my eyes off her.

The wolfhound looked as if he was in pain as he twirled her around. He lowered her to the floor. That was when she saw me.

"Sly," she squealed. "I knew you would come."

"Lotta," I said. "I wouldn't think of missing your opening night. Everyone from our barnyard days will be here to cheer for you." I handed her the chocolates.

"You remembered," she said, smiling. "Come quickly, everyone. I want you to meet my dear friend, and very clever private investigator, Sly, P.I."

The others gathered around us.

"This is Yuri Wolfruff," said Lotta. "He is the prince in the ballet."

I nodded.

"And this is Mimi Meow. She is the evil fairy and my understudy," Lotta said.

I smiled at Mimi. Heigh-ho, was that a look of envy I saw on Mimi's face? I asked myself.

"Come. Walk me to my dressing room," said Lotta, pulling me along.

We climbed the narrow stairs to Lotta's room. A musician rushed by us. He nearly knocked me over with his cello case.

"Things have changed since our days on the farm. But I still love these chocolates," Lotta said as she munched on one.

I watched as a small piece of chocolate fell to the floor. In a wink, she had it scooped up and safely back in her mouth. I laughed.

"I remember how Messy-Face Elmo Rat stood by, waiting for you to drop a bit of food. You were so fast. He never had a chance. You made him furious."

"I was a runt. I needed that food," said Lotta. "Anyway, he was always sneaking around stealing food from the others."

"That's why his face was a mess all the time," I said.

We laughed at the thought.

"I just want the hometown to be proud of me tonight," said Lotta.

"You'll be great," I told her. "As they say in the theater: 'Break a leg.'"

Missing Toe Shoes
·2·

I left Lotta at her dressing-room door and started down the hallway. She came running after me, shouting, "They're gone! They're gone!"

"What's gone?" I asked.

"All of my toe shoes are gone," said Lotta.

Maestro Gander heard the noise. He came to see what was wrong. "Oh, n-n-n-no," he moaned. "What shall we d-d-d-do? It's almost time for the b-b-b-ballet to begin."

"No need to worry. Sly, P.I., here," I said. "I will have this case solved in no time."

I searched the dressing rooms. I searched the stage area. I searched the orchestra pit. Not a toe shoe was found.

On my way back to Lotta's dressing room, I saw Mimi holding something in her hand.

"Heigh-ho, what's this?" I asked Mimi.

"I found this lying in the hallway," she said as she gave it to me.

"That's a satin ribbon from one of my toe shoes," cried Lotta.

All eyes were on Mimi.

I thought for a moment. I remembered the look of envy on Mimi's face when we met. "Isn't it true that you are Lotta's understudy?" I asked.

"Yes, but..." she began.

"Aren't you a little jealous of Lotta?" I asked.

"Yes, but..."

"If Lotta doesn't dance, who would dance for her?" I asked.

"I would," Mimi answered. "But I wouldn't. I couldn't. I didn't." She began to cry.

"Stop!" shouted Maestro. "Y-Y-Y-You are upsetting my d-d-d-dancers. Everyone, to your r-r-r-rooms."

I wanted to ask more questions. But before I had a chance, there was a terrifying scream.

I rushed to Lotta's dressing room.

"A man! My costumes!" she shrieked,
pointing to the open window. Then she
fainted—on me.

· 23 ·

Sly to the Rescue

·3·

By the time I had gotten out from under Lotta, the man and her costumes were long gone. I looked out Lotta's window. A ledge ran along the side of the building, leading to an open window.

I went next door. It was Yuri's dressing room. I found him stuffing something into a bag. He looked up and tried to hide it.

"Heigh-ho, what's going on?" I asked.

Lotta and Maestro came into Yuri's room.

"Were you in your room a few moments ago?" I asked.

"No," answered Yuri.

"Where were you?"

Yuri was silent.

"This room was the only escape for the thief. What are you hiding there?" I asked.

Yuri looked at Maestro and Lotta. "Nothing," he said.

I remembered how pained Yuri looked as he lifted Lotta into the air. "Isn't it true it is hard for you to lift Lotta?"

Yuri nodded. "Lotta is very light on her feet, but she is not very light to lift."

"Well, really!" said Lotta in disgust.

"If something happened to stop Lotta from dancing, you would dance with Mimi. That would be much easier for you. Isn't that true?" I asked.

"Yes," said Yuri. "But I did not take her things."

"Where were you, then?"

Mimi came into the room. "He was with me."

"Heigh-ho, perhaps you are in this together," I said.

"Oh m·m-m-my," muttered Maestro. "What n-n-n-next?"

"We had nothing to do with Lotta's missing things," said Mimi.

"Tell me," I said. "What are you hiding in the bag?"

Yuri and Mimi looked at Maestro and Lotta.

"Show us," I said.

"Yes, do show us," said Lotta.

Yuri slowly opened the bag.

Everyone waited.

"Flowers?" I said in surprise.

"Yes," Yuri answered. "On opening night, Maestro sends everyone flowers for good luck. They make Mimi and me sneeze.

We wanted to get rid of them without Maestro knowing."

"A simple explanation," I said.

"But my costumes and toe shoes are still missing," sobbed Lotta. "Please, Sly, help me. Where are they? Who took them?" Huge tears rolled down Lotta's cheeks. "I must go on. This is our hometown. I want everyone to be proud of me. Don't let my opening night end like this," begged Lotta.

Maestro hugged Lotta. "I h-h-h-hope, Sly, P.I., you are as good as you s-s-s-say. T-T-T-Time is running out."

"I must think," I said.

Rats in the Basement

· 4 ·

I went over everything that had happened that night. Suddenly an eerie sound interrupted my thoughts. "Heigh-ho, what's that?"

The sound echoed through the air vent.

"Where does this vent lead to?" I asked.

"The basement," answered Maestro.

"To the basement!" I cried.

Maestro led the way. I followed. Lotta, Yuri and Mimi were close behind. The sound grew louder as we neared the basement.

"Heigh-ho, it sounds like a lullaby," I said as I pulled the door open. The singing stopped. And there in the shadows was one of Lotta's shoes swinging back and forth from a water pipe.

"My toe shoe," cried Lotta.

I turned on the light. Before us stood two scared rats.

"What is the meaning of this?" asked one of the rats. "Why are you disturbing our home?"

"Allow me to introduce myself. I am Sly, P.I. I am investigating the theft of Miss Oink's toe shoes and costumes."

"Miss Lotta Oink? The world famous ballerina?" asked the other rat.

"Yes," I said. "And that toe shoe is one that was missing."

"Oh, no," said the first rat. "Mrs. Ratatat and I want to see Miss Oink dance."

"So you stole my toe shoe?" asked Lotta.

"We did not steal it," said Mr. Ratatat. "We found it lying in the hallway. One satin ribbon was missing, so we thought it was being thrown away."

"As you can see," said Mrs. Ratatat, gently pushing the toe shoe, "it is a perfect crib for our babies. They will sleep tight while we watch Miss Oink dance."

"You have no other shoes?" I asked.

"Only this one," said Mrs. Ratatat.

Maestro Gander looked at his watch. "T-T-T-Time has run out. The b-b-b-ballet must begin. M-M-M-Mimi, you will have to take Lotta's place."

"No! No! No!" yelled Lotta. "Sly, do something!" And she dashed up the stairs.

A Trapped Rat

· 5 ·

Lotta ran wildly down the hallway. She rammed into a musician. They both fell to the floor. Maestro helped Lotta to her feet. I helped the musician pick up his cello case.

Heigh-ho, I thought. Isn't this the same musician that nearly knocked me over earlier? "Shouldn't you be in the orchestra pit?" I asked him.

"He does not b-b-b-belong here," said Maestro. "He is not in the orchestra."

I looked carefully at the musician. "Do you mind if I look at your instrument?" I asked as I put my hands on the cello case.

"Yeah, I do," he said.

He tugged. I pulled. We struggled.

Suddenly, the case burst open. Toe shoes and costumes flew everywhere.

"Call the police," I yelled.

The musician tried to run. Being not only clever, but fast, I stopped him.

I reached over and pulled the mustache off
his face.

"Yeow!" he cried.

"Just as I thought," I said. "Messy-Face
Elmo!"

"Messy-Face Elmo!" squealed Lotta.

"Yeah, it's me," he snarled.

"Why did you take my things?" cried Lotta. "What have I ever done to you?"

Messy-Face Elmo's beady eyes glared at Lotta. "Because you're a pig!" he shouted. "You never shared any of your food with me. You gobbled it all up. I got nothing. You always had the best of everything, and now you're a big star. It's not fair!"

Lotta sputtered, "Well, I never."

"I wanted to make you pay for never sharing anything with me," snarled Messy-Face Elmo. "I knew how important tonight was to you. With no toe shoes or costumes, you would not have been able to dance. My plan would have worked if Sly hadn't come along. He ruined everything."

"I always knew you were a disgusting rat," Lotta sniffed.

Case Solved

· 6 ·

The police came and took Messy-Face
Elmo away. He kept yelling, "I'll get you for
this, Sly, P.I."

I wasn't worried. Lotta had her toe shoes and costumes back. The ballet was about to begin.

"You are so clever, Sly," said Lotta. "How did you know it was Messy-Face Elmo?"

"Simple," I said. "Messy-Face Elmo could never pass up anything good to eat. His mustache was a chocolate mess."

"P-P-P-Places, everyone," shouted Maestro.

"Break a leg," I told Lotta, and headed for the balcony. I took my seat in the Opera House and waited for the curtain to rise.

Heigh-ho, I said to myself, another case solved.